FREDDIE'S
AMAZING BAKERY

THE GREAT RASPBERRY MIX-UP

WRITTEN BY
HARRIET WHITEHORN

OXFORD
UNIVERSITY PRESS

ILLUSTRATED BY
ALEX G GRIFFITHS

Our story is set in a town called *Belville* —look, here is a map of it. As you can see, it is a delightful place, just the right size, and criss-crossed by a spider's web of pretty canals (perfect for boating in summer and skating in winter), which are lined with cherry trees and tall old houses.

MAGNOLIA CANAL

BELVILLE THEATRE

BELVILLE MUSEUM

Belville is the sort of town
that **LOVES** a celebration so:

♥ In winter, when the first snow falls,
all the townspeople gather in the main
square and drink hot punch, eat
ginger cake, and wish each other a
happy winter.

♥ In the spring time, when the cherry
trees **BURST** into floaty pink blossom,
each canal holds a street party to
celebrate.

♥ Then on the longest day of the year
in the summer, everyone gathers for
a barbeque in the park and stays up
late playing games and letting off
fireworks.

♥ And in the autumn . . . well actually,
in the autumn there aren't any kinds of
party or celebration, and since autumn
can be a bit sad, what with all the
leaves falling off the trees, and it

getting dark so early in the evening, everyone was **DELIGHTED** when Mrs Van de Lune, of Van de Lune's Hotel (quite the grandest hotel in Belville) decided to hold a baking competition–for what could be JOLLIER than that?!

And here's the poster for it:

Belville
BAKING COMPETITON

with special judges
Mrs Van de Lune & Monsieur Brioche

£500 PRIZE
THEME: *Belville!*

SATURDAY 10AM at the VAN DE LUNE HOTEL,

ALL ENTRIES WELCOME

ALL CONTESTANTS TO PROVIDE OWN INGREDIENTS

As you can see from the poster, anyone is allowed to enter, and the theme for the cakes is Belville itself. The competition is to be held at the hotel and will be judged by Mrs Van de Lune and the hotel patisserie chef, Monsieur Brioche. And there is £500 prize money for the winner.

Now, if you look at the map, you can see over on the right FREDDIE'S AMAZING BAKERY. It isn't a LARGE shop—in fact you would probably say it was pretty SMALL. Nor is it in a FASHIONABLE part of the town. But no one cares because the

cakes and pastries are SO delicious
and the bakery looks SO pretty,
covered as it is in paintings of
flowers and animals. And this is where
our story starts, at Freddie's, the day
before the competition . . .

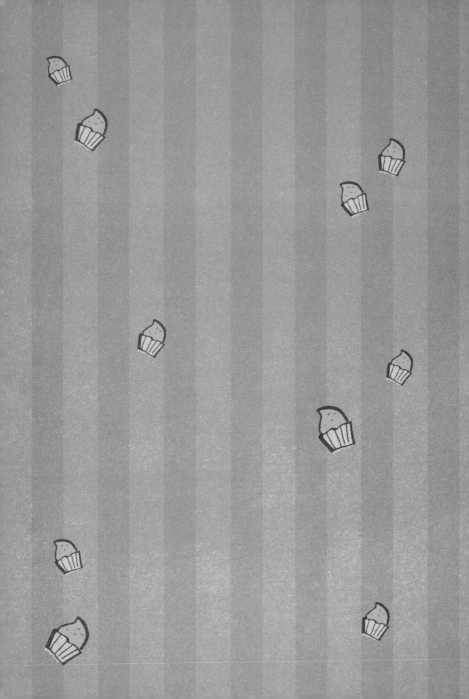

CHAPTER ONE

It was five o'clock in the morning and all Belville was asleep. And, in a cosy bed at the very top of a tall, scruffy old house, our young hero, Freddie, was dreaming of cake. And not just any cake—oh no, this was a real showstopper, a cake good enough to win the baking competition.

BRRIIINGG! went Freddie's alarm clock—because bakers have to get up **REALLY** early in the morning.

Freddie was awake in the click of a finger, and before he forgot a single, tiny detail of his dream, he reached for his special red CAKE notebook which he always kept with him, put on his glasses, and made a quick sketch of it. And then, because he had a busy day ahead, Freddie **LEAPT** out of bed and got on with his morning routine, which went like this:

1 Wake up Flapjack, his French bulldog, by giving him a good **TICKLE**.

2 Kung fu practice (in pyjamas) for half an hour.

3 A quick bath and a slow careful teeth brushing (very important when you eat a lot of cake).

4 Get dressed in baker's uniform—a smart white jacket and some rather natty trousers. He had a special pocket in the jacket for his CAKE notebook.

5 Hair combing—the **WORST** part of the morning for Freddie, as he had that stubborn sort of hair that will not lie flat however much you torture or beg it. He usually gave up and shoved his baker's hat on his head.

6 And then the **BEST** bit . . . the baker's chute! It was in fact an old laundry chute, but that didn't matter to Freddie. With Flapjack on his lap, Freddie slid down, **TWIRLING** round and round like a helter-skelter, all the way down to his shop and kitchen on the ground floor of the building.

And now, I'd like to introduce you to someone else—Amira.

Amira has caramel-coloured skin, kind brown eyes, and SWOOSHY black hair that is always tied neatly back. As well as being Freddie's best friend, she also manages the bakery for him.

'Good morning Amira, you're in early. Is everything OK?' Freddie asked.

Amira was sitting at the table, with her glasses on, adding up rows of numbers. She sighed a little before replying, 'I was just working out if we could afford to buy a new cooker.'

The cooker was very old and much too small for all the baking that Freddie needed to do.

'And can we?' Freddie asked hopefully.

'I'm afraid not,' Amira replied, but then gave Freddie a big smile. 'Unless you win the baking competition!'

'That'll never happen,' Freddie said modestly.

'Nonsense!' Amira exclaimed. 'You're easily the best baker in Belville.'

'What about Monsieur Brioche? He's brilliant,' Freddie said.

'He's not as good as you!' Amira said. 'And besides, he can't enter a competition that he's judging. Have you decided on a design for your cake yet?'

'I have,' Freddie replied. He pulled out his book and showed her the sketch.

'**Wow!**' Amira gasped. 'The carousel in the park—that's a brilliant idea! And I love the raspberry theme—**DELICIOUS**! And that brilliant raspberry food colouring from the Baker's Emporium will give it a perfect colour too. It's really great, Freddie.'

'Do you think so?' Freddie said, looking uncertain. 'I was really pleased with the design, but now I'm worrying that perhaps it's a bit complicated and difficult . . .'

Now, as you may have noticed, Freddie was rather lacking in confidence. So thank goodness he had a best friend like Amira who always made him feel better about himself. In fact, it was Amira who had encouraged Freddie to open the shop in the first place and persuaded him to name it 'FREDDIE'S AMAZING BAKERY'.

'Honestly Freddie,' Amira said, looking at the sketch, 'the cake will be **FANTASTIC!** Monsieur Brioche and Mrs Van de Lune are going to love it.'

Freddie smiled—Amira always made him feel better.

'Are you going to make a practice cake beforehand?' she asked.

'I think I should have time this afternoon, once I've done all the deliveries,' he replied.

'I can't wait to see it,' Amira said. 'Now I'd better just go and tidy the shop—it'll be opening time before we know it!'

Just before eight o'clock, Freddie stopped baking to take everything from the kitchen through to the shop. Amira came and helped.

'Those lemon tarts look fab, Freddie!' said Amira, picking up a tray of them. 'They're a great colour.'

'I added a little pink grapefruit to them,' Freddie said. 'And try some of this gateaux—I've made it mint chocolate for a change.'

Amira took a bite. 'Mmm delicious!' she exclaimed.

Amira and Freddie carefully arranged all the tarts and cakes, croissants and other goodies before Freddie raised the blinds on the shop window and door. There was already a long queue of people, who all

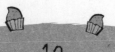

cheered when they saw Freddie change the CLOSED sign to OPEN.

'Good morning!' Freddie said, opening the door and welcoming the first people into the shop with a happy smile. Another day at **FREDDIE'S AMAZING BAKERY** had begun.

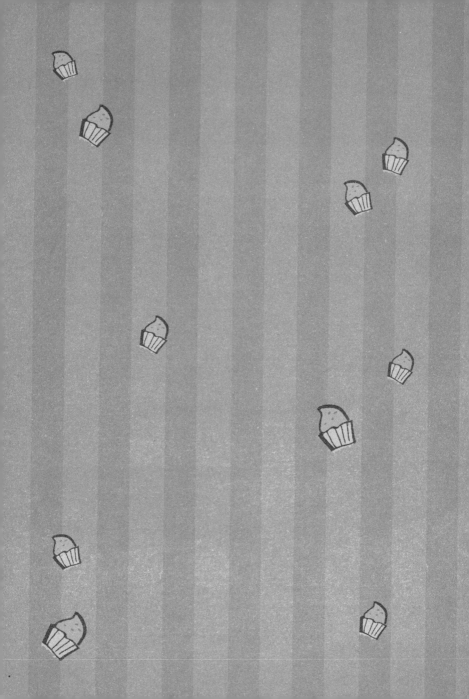

CHAPTER TWO

It's now time for you to meet another baker—his name is Bernard Macaroon, and his shop, which his grandfather started, is called Macaroon's Patisserie. If you look at the map, you can see that it is right in the centre of Belville. It has a **BIG** shiny glass shop front and lots of flashing signs, despite which, the shop is never

very full because although there is
nothing really wrong with the cakes, as
Bernard always follows his grandfather's
recipes **VERY PRECISELY**, they are just
rather boring, or you could say, if you
were being a bit mean . . . tasteless.

Anyway, on the morning that our
story begins, Bernard was in the kitchen,
brandishing a silver ruler like a sword,
shouting at a row of frightened young
men and women, who were dressed in
the purple and black patisserie uniform.
He looked like a furious general
inspecting his troops . . .

'No wonder my shop is empty!' he
bellowed, his large brown eyes popping.

'You, what's-your-name!' he said, pointing his ruler at an unfortunate young man. 'Your trousers are two centimetres too long, and your hair is one centimetre over your collar! And the croissants you made this morning were fifteen centimetres long instead of fourteen! You're a disgrace!!'

The poor boy looked as if he were about to cry.

'Now I am going to my office where I will be incredibly busy, and no one is to bother me for exactly forty-one minutes.'

Bernard turned to go, but then something unexpected happened. One of Bernard's waitresses plucked up the courage to speak. Her name was Sophie, and she was small, with neat blonde hair and curious hazel eyes.

'Excuse me, sir, but I've had an idea,' Sophie said.

'An idea?!' Bernard spun round and looked at her as if she were mad. 'What sort of idea?'

'An idea for the shop,' she replied calmly. 'Let me explain. I was very hungry after work yesterday, so I stopped at **FREDDIE'S AMAZING BAKERY** and bought myself a sausage roll. It was absolutely delicious because he uses cheesy pastry and adds lots of herbs and spices to the meat, and I just thought that we could consider doing this to our sausage rolls to give them a bit more flavour. And then I bought one of his almond tarts and it was really yummy. I think it's because he puts a thick layer of apricot jam . . .'

Bernard could bear it no longer—he was so angry that he thought his head might EXPLODE.

'You are wrong! And he is wrong too!' he shouted rudely at poor Sophie. 'Apricot jam does NOT belong in an almond tart any more than herbs and spices belong in a sausage roll! Everything made in this patisserie is made as it should be, following the correct recipes. Everything Freddie makes has been fiddled about with and tastes WRONG! Do you understand me?!'

'Yes,' Sophie squeaked.

'Good!' Bernard replied. 'Now get on with your work. And if anyone else has any bright ideas, I don't want to hear them!'

Bernard stomped into his office, **SLAMMING** the door and waking up his cat, Otto, who was snoozing on an armchair. The cat opened one eye and glared at Bernard. He had been in the middle of a really good dream.

Now, just a word about Otto. Bernard
had named him after his father, who
had been a rather good-looking man,
and Otto had indeed been a very sweet-
looking kitten, but now . . . not so
much. He was **VAST**, with a tummy that
swung along beneath him as if it had a
life of its own, short stubby little legs,
and a grumpy, squished-up face, with
spiteful green eyes. And at this precise
moment, those eyes were fixed on
Bernard, who was pacing up and down,
ranting furiously.

'All I ever hear is Freddie this! Freddie
that! Oh Freddie, he's so a-mazing!'
Bernard took a deep breath trying to

calm himself. 'I'm going to show that stupid boy, and everyone else, who is the best baker in Belville once and for all! I'm going to win that baking competition!' he vowed.

Bernard was very pleased with his cake idea which was a precisely measured copy of Van de Lune's Hotel. Bernard would stop at nothing in order to suck up to Mrs Van de Lune.

'She will definitely make me the winner,' Bernard told himself. But then a little of voice of doubt said, 'What if she doesn't? What if Freddie wins?'

Even the thought of this was too much for Bernard to bear.

'I am going to win the competition!' he repeated through clenched teeth and then added, 'Even if I have to cheat to do so!'

The idea of cheating made Bernard feel much better. He loved cheating and he was really good at it. Now all he had to do was think of a plan.

'If only I knew what design Freddie was making! Then I could think of how to ruin it!'

An image of Freddie's red CAKE notebook popped into Bernard's head. He'd seen it sticking out of Freddie's jacket pocket many times.

'I need to get a look in that notebook!' Bernard exclaimed. But that was easier said than done. After much umming and ahhing, and sighing and tugging at his beard, Bernard finally

came up with a plan. It wasn't a very
good one, but anyway, this was it:

Bernard would stand outside
his shop waiting for Freddie to
cycle past when he was doing his
deliveries.

Bernard would **SHOVE** Otto in front
of Freddie's bicycle making Freddie
fall off his bicycle.

When Freddie fell off his bicycle, his
red notebook was likely to fall out of
his pocket.

Bernard would then **STEAL** the
notebook while pretending to help
Freddie.

Well, I told you it wasn't a very good plan (and frankly a bit mean to Otto) but there you go, that was Bernard for you. He was **DELIGHTED** with it. He  glanced at his watch. He had about an hour before Freddie would be passing on his deliveries. Easily enough time to work out the details, he thought, smiling his big shark-like smile.

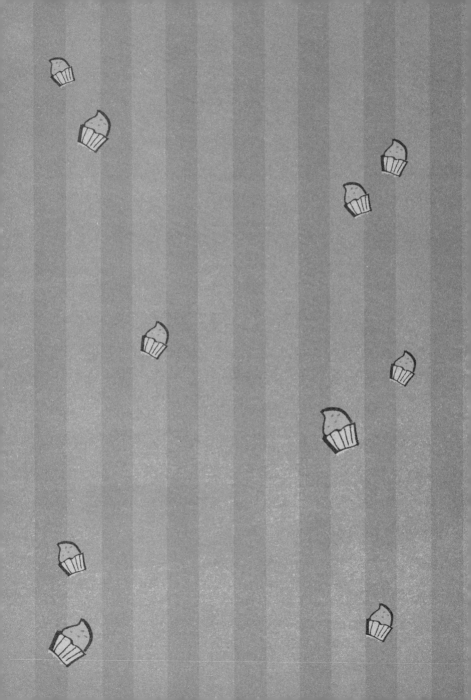

CHAPTER THREE

Meanwhile, back at Freddie's the morning rush was over, and Freddie was busy baking.

First he made meringues, then he iced the birthday cakes that people had ordered. He injected cream into piles of profiteroles and filled the eclairs, which were the bakery's speciality (not only did he make chocolate, but coffee, caramel,

and strawberry, too!). Then he made
a **MOUNTAIN** of cookies and a troop of
chocolate mice.

'How are you getting on?' Amira asked
as Freddie brought all the trays of yummy
things into the shop.

'All done for now,' Freddie replied. 'So
I'm going to go and make the deliveries.'

Most people in Belville walked or cycled
around the town and Freddie was no
exception. It was one of his favourite
parts of the day, cycling around Belville
delivering cakes—he had lots of friends
and often bumped into them.

His first stop was the café in the park,
which was perfect as it gave him the

chance to have another look at the carousel. He cycled up Main Canal waving to the shopkeepers as he went. His friend Samuel, who ran the bookshop, called out, 'See you tomorrow, Freddie!' Samuel was entering the baking competition too.

'See you tomorrow and good luck!' Freddie called back.

And then Freddie cycled past Macaroon's Patisserie. Bernard was standing outside, holding Otto, and well, you know what was going to happen. When Freddie wasn't looking, poor Otto got **SHOVED** in front of the bicycle.

But Freddie didn't fall off—he braked and SWERVED neatly to avoid Otto and somehow managed to stop his deliveries toppling out of the trailer on the back of his bicycle. Flapjack, who was sitting in the basket on the front of the bike, started to bark at Otto, as if to say, 'What on earth do you think you're doing?'

Otto, who understandably, was not in the best mood, hissed loudly back.

'Flapjack! Be quiet!' Freddie said, and then exclaimed, 'I'm SO sorry Bernard! Thank goodness I didn't hit your poor cat.'

Now Bernard was feeling pretty cross that his plan hadn't worked and Freddie's notebook was still safe in his pocket, so he decided to make Freddie feel really bad.

'You should look where you're going! My poor Otto!' he cried, bending down to the cat, who hissed at him too. 'He's clearly not in his right mind, he's so upset.'

'I really am very sorry,' Freddie apologized again. 'Is there anything I can do to make it up to you?'

It didn't take Bernard long to reply.

'Well yes, Freddie, there is something actually. Could I look at your notebook?' he asked smoothly. 'I have always admired it and I wanted to get one just like it.'

'Er, yes OK,' Freddie replied, thinking it was a slightly odd thing to ask. He pulled the notebook out of his pocket and handed it to Bernard. To be honest, if Bernard had asked, Freddie would have told him what cake he was making for the competition anyway—it wasn't a secret.

Bernard pretended to admire the cover, then flicked through the pages, lingering over the most recent drawing of the carousel. **DRAT!** He thought, furiously, *that's such a good idea!* But then an evil plan began to hatch in his mind . . . He gave Freddie a grin and handed the notebook back, saying, 'Thank you so much and best of luck for tomorrow!'

'Good luck to you too,' Freddie replied politely, putting the notebook back in his pocket. 'And I'm so sorry again about your cat.'

'Oh, don't worry!' Bernard said breezily.

As Freddie cycled away, he whispered, 'That was a bit strange wasn't it, Flapjack?'

The residents of Belville didn't like to boast but they did all agree that they had one of the nicest parks imaginable. There were wide lawns full of springy grass, pretty flowerbeds, and a large lake that you could go boating on. And best of all, next to the lake was the old-fashioned carousel that Freddie wanted to copy for his cake.

Freddie stopped to look at it as it turned round and round. It was full of happy children, laughing and waving, as the horses went up and down to the music.

It really is a beautiful shade of raspberry pink, Freddie thought, *and then there are those lovely painted roses around the middle which I could make in fondant icing, and the horses too. The gold twirly bits on the tops could be in marzipan, and then I could make the horses' poles out of candy canes . . .*

He took out his notebook and scribbled a few more notes. But there wasn't time to think too much about the competition; Freddie had lots of customers to think about first, so he got back on his bike and delivered . . .

a dozen assorted cakes to the café in the park

fifteen lemon tarts to the museum

twenty-one coffee eclairs to the ballet dancers at the theatre

a magnificent fruit gateau to Madame Bolkowski at 4 Green Canal who was having a grand party that night.

And then he made a brief stop at the fruit stall in Market Square to buy a large box of raspberries. At the stall, he bumped into his friend, Jojo. She loved baking too and had also entered the competition.

'Hello Freddie,' she said. 'I'm just buying the apples for the apple tart I'm making tomorrow.'

'Ooh YUM! I love apple tart,' Freddie replied, licking his lips. 'And what a good idea. Belville is really famous for its apples.'

'Well, it seemed like a good idea, but whenever I make the tart it comes out with a soggy bottom! I feel really bad asking you but have you got any tips?'

Freddie laughed. 'Soggy bottoms can be a big problem!' he joked. 'Have you tried baking the pastry first with no filling in it?'

Jojo shook her head.

'Try that then—it should work,' Freddie said.

'Thank you so much!' Jojo replied.

'It's my pleasure,' Freddie said, smiling.

But we need to leave them chatting in the market because . . . oh no! Something is happening back at the AMAZING BAKERY . . .

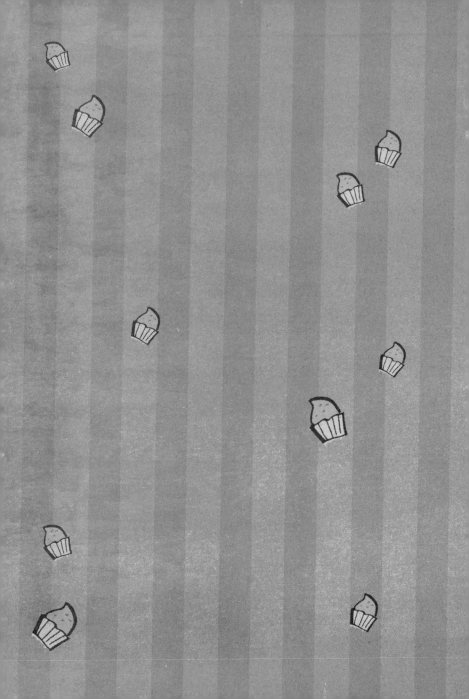

CHAPTER FOUR

Amira was rushed off her feet serving in the shop and didn't notice someone suspicious-looking had come in the back door of the kitchen and had started digging around in the cupboards. Uh oh!

Who is it and what do they want? I can't quite see, can you? Freddie needs to get back . . . **QUICK!** But he doesn't know he has an intruder in the kitchen and is far too busy delivering birthday cakes . . .

a chocolate one for Ayesha Patel at 12 Magnolia Canal

a vanilla one for Marlie Mayes at Apartment 4, 3 Water Lane

a strawberry one for Su Lin at 6 Flower Canal.

He was just cycling home when he passed the dog shelter which was run by his friend, Mrs Mackenzie. Flapjack had come from there when he was a puppy, and both he and Freddie loved going to

see Mrs Mackenzie and
all the other dogs.
Freddie knew that she
was entering the cake
competition too, and he
was just wondering if he had
time to stop and say hello and see how she
was getting on, when he noticed that the
front gate to the shelter was slightly open.
And when he looked closer, he spotted a
little furry, cream-coloured dog poking its
face out, considering whether to escape.

'Oh no you don't!' Freddie said, stopping
and parking his bicycle. He scooped up the
little dog and lifted Flapjack down from his
basket. Then he went inside the gate and
rang the doorbell.

Mrs Mackenzie answered it a moment

later, looking rather stressed.

'Hello!' Freddie greeted her. 'I'm afraid someone had left your gate open and look who I found, trying to escape!'

'Oh no!' Mrs Mackenzie groaned. 'Thank you so much! Come on Tinkerbell, back to the garden where you belong. Will you come in for a moment, Freddie, and see all the new dogs that have arrived?'

Freddie and Flapjack followed her through to the big garden at the back of the house. There was a large crowd of dogs and Flapjack, tail wagging furiously, bounded off to join them while Freddie and Mrs Mackenzie stood and watched.

'They're so sweet, aren't they?' Freddie said, watching all the dogs gambolling around.

'I know,' Mrs Mackenzie replied. 'But I'm really worried, Freddie. We have so many dogs to look after, but the shelter has practically run out of money. If we don't get some more soon, we may have to shut.'

'That's terrible!' Freddie cried.

'It is indeed,' Mrs Mackenzie sighed.
'And just to add to my troubles, I'm
having a nightmare with my entry for the
baking competition! As you know, I'm
only entering to create some publicity for
the shelter. I know I haven't a hope of
actually winning, but equally I don't want
to make a complete fool of myself! I've
been practising my cake for days, but I
just can't seem to get it right. It's based on
the cherry blossom and it always ends up
looking like a big pink mess!'

'Shall I come and have a look? Perhaps
I might be able to give you some advice?'
Freddie offered.

'But that doesn't seem fair, Freddie,
you're in the competition too. You

probably shouldn't be helping out another competitor,' Mrs Mackenzie said.

'Honestly, I don't mind,' Freddie replied.

'Well, that's very kind of you,' Mrs Mackenzie said, leading him off to the the kitchen.

Oh dear! The pink cake did indeed look a bit of a mess.

'What you are trying to do is really difficult,' Freddie reassured Mrs Mackenzie. 'But the cherry blossom is a great idea. Have you thought about making it all in biscuit instead?'

'Is that allowed?' Mrs Mackenzie asked, looking doubtful.

'Yes, definitely. It says on the posters you can make a cake or a tart or biscuits. It doesn't matter so long as it's baked. And if you did it in biscuit, you could make a trunk quite easily with a rectangular cutter and then get a flower biscuit cutter from the Baker's Emporium. Then you just have to do pink icing petals with a yellow centre.' He got out his notebook and did her a quick sketch.

Mrs Mackenzie looked delighted. 'Oh, Freddie, you are so kind. Thank you.'

'It's a pleasure. And now I'd better get on as I need to practise my cake too.'

'Of course. See you tomorrow,' said Mrs Mackenzie with a big smile. 'And thank you again, Freddie.'

Freddie returned to his bakery but whoever had been sneaking around in the kitchen had disappeared long ago. Goodness knows what they were doing in there, but I'm sure we'll find out soon enough . . .

Freddie put on his apron, washed his hands, and took a deep breath. Then he began.

First he made three vanilla sponge cakes for the base, middle, and roof of the carousel, adding most of the raspberries he had bought right before he put the cakes in the oven. And then, while they were cooking . . .

He **BOILED** some sugar and made the twirly horses' poles.

He **MIXED** the rest of the raspberries with buttercream to make a filling to sandwich the sponges together.

He made some **MARZIPAN** for the gold decorations on the top.

Then he **WHIPPED** up some fondant icing for the horses and the roses.

He was halfway through moulding them when the timer went **'PING!'** telling him that the cakes were ready. He took them out of oven to cool.

After that he made a large amount

of thick royal icing to cover the carousel. But when Freddie went to look for his raspberry pink food colouring, he found that the bottle was missing.

That's strange, he thought to himself. *I used it this morning for the pink meringues. Never mind, I'll just have to leave the cake white and then go out and buy some more.*

Then Freddie began the really fun bit—assembling everything to make the carousel.

And once all that was done, he added the final touches—he stuck on the roses and the carousel horses.

Freddie worked away quite happily and just as the clock was striking five, he was done.

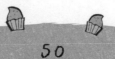

'Two hours exactly!' Amira said, coming into the kitchen. She looked at the carousel and cried, 'What a **MASTERPIECE!** Well done, Freddie!'

'Thank you!' he replied. 'But it needs to be pink. Strangely, I can't find the raspberry pink food colouring anywhere. I'll go out and get some more in a minute, but let's just taste the cake first.'

He cut into it, and Amira and he tried each bit of the carousel.

'**DELICIOUS!**' Amira announced.

'I think it's OK,' Freddie said modestly, because the cake really was **SCRUMPTIOUS**. 'It'll be better with the added raspberry flavouring.' Then he glanced at the clock. 'I'd better get going.'

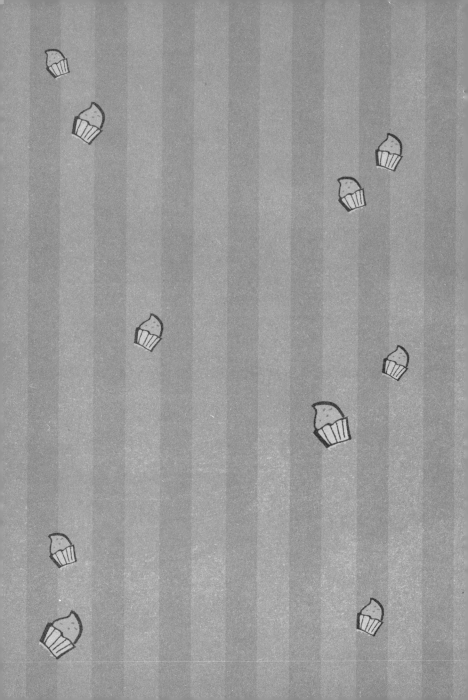

CHAPTER FIVE

Freddie hopped on his bike and cycled off to the Baker's Emporium. But although they had every other food colouring imaginable, they had sold out of all the pink food colouring.

Oh well, he thought, *I'll just have to try somewhere else.* But it was the same at the next shop, and the next . . . all poor Freddie heard was:

'I'm so sorry . . .'

'Oh no! I just sold the last bottle an hour ago . . .'

'If you'd only come in earlier . . .'

What a **CATASTROPHE!** It was nearly seven o'clock, and Freddie was beginning to panic as he cycled across Market Square. All the stalls were packing up for the night, and he glanced around in desperation. He could hardly believe his eyes when he saw a large sign saying

FOOD COLOURING FOR SALE.

This was certainly his lucky day! He cycled straight over.

It wasn't really a proper stall—there was just someone who appeared to be a very elderly gentleman sitting in a chair, bundled up in a hat, scarf, and coat,

which was strange because the weather
was quite warm. It was hard to see his
face as he had a large moustache and
bushy beard and he was wearing dark
glasses.

'Good evening!' Freddie greeted the man. 'I don't suppose you have any pink food colouring, do you?'

'You're in luck! I do indeed young man,' he replied in a strange croaky voice with a thick foreign accent. He rummaged around in a box and pulled out a small glass bottle.

'Here it is. Now I have to tell you this is very special—it comes from the extremely rare Pinkolla raspberries that only grow high up in the Atlas mountains of Morocco. It gives the most **BEAUTIFUL** pink colour.'

'Really?' Freddie exclaimed excitedly. 'Does it taste of raspberries too?'

'Deliciously so,' the old man said. 'It is used to flavour the raspberry jam that the sultan eats on his toast every day for his breakfast.'

'That's perfect!' Freddie cried. 'It's just what I need for the competition!'

'What an amazing coincidence.' The old man smiled, a little like a shark, and Flapjack gave a growl.

Freddie thanked the man and paid him.

I can't believe my luck, he thought as he cycled home.

So, the day of the competition has arrived! It starts at ten o'clock in the morning, and I don't know about you, but I am feeling rather nervous for Freddie. Look! Here he comes with all

his ingredients in a big box strapped to
the back of his bike . . .

*It seems like the whole of Belville has turned
out to watch the competition,* Freddie
thought nervously as he walked onto
the stage and saw the sea of faces in the
audience. He spotted Amira near the
front, with Flapjack. She smiled at him
and mouthed 'good luck'. Freddie tried
not to feel too scared as he got out all
his ingredients. He was pleased to see
Mrs Mackenzie next to him, and he said
hello and good luck to the other three
contestants—Samuel, Jojo, and, of course,
Bernard. They all wished him cheery good
lucks back, including Bernard, who was

looking particularly pleased with himself.

Mrs Van de Lune walked onto the stage with Monsieur Brioche. She was a tall, elegant lady, with an air of calm about her, while Monsieur Brioche was small and dark, and was one of those people who get very excited about everything and wave their hands around a lot.

'Welcome everyone to Belville's first ever baking competition,' Mrs Van de Lune announced. 'Now contestants, you have two hours to bake a cake—any sort of cake or tart or biscuits—that best sums up Belville for you. Now, if you're all prepared . . . Ready . . . steady . . . BAKE!'

'Good luck to you all! And may the best baker win!!' Monsieur Brioche cried in his thick French accent.

Freddie had written out his method— it looked like this:

- Make the sponge cakes.
- Make the sugar canes for the horses' poles.
- Make the marzipan and mould into the decorations for the top.
- Make the buttercream filling.
- Make the raspberry pink royal icing.
- Make the fondant icing for the horses and roses.
- Assemble.

Freddie worked quickly, and soon the cakes were in the oven, the poles were twisted, and the marzipan decorations finished. He had just made the buttercream when his timer went off, telling him that the sponges were done. He went over to his oven to get the cakes out . . . But, oh no!

'Someone's turned my oven off!' Freddie cried.

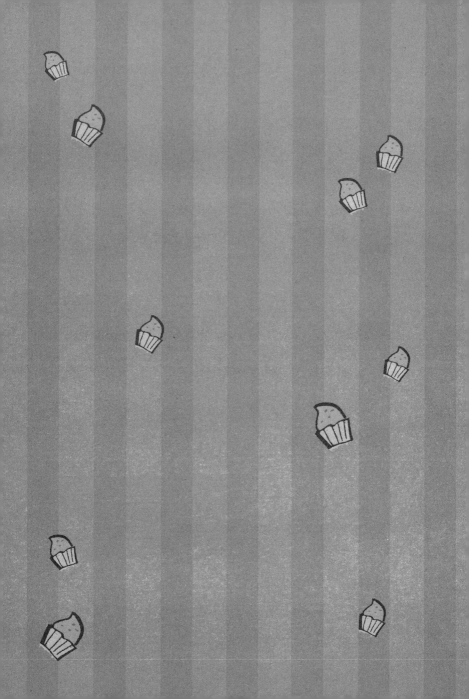

CHAPTER
SIX

Mrs Van de Lune came straight over.

'Oh no!' she cried. 'Are you sure you turned it on in the first place?'

'Absolutely!' Freddie replied. 'Look, it's still a little bit warm.'

'Yes, it would appear that someone has definitely turned it off,' Mrs Van de Lune agreed.

Who would have done such a thing? Freddie looked over at the other contestants. Everyone was busy baking, except for Bernard who saw Freddie glancing over at him and then immediately looked away, a sly smile on his face.

Freddie sighed and looked at the half-baked cakes. They would be horrible if he tried to bake them for longer now. **What a disaster!**

'I'll have to start again,' Freddie said with a heavy sigh.

'Do you have enough ingredients?' Mrs Van de Lune asked.

He thought for a moment. 'Just about,' he replied.

'And will you be able to finish in time?' she asked.

Freddie sighed again. 'Probably not,' he said.

'Well, just do what you can, and good luck,' said Mrs Van de Lune. Then she clapped her hands and announced, 'One hour is up, ladies and gentlemen. You have another one to go.'

Freddie glanced at Amira in the audience who mouthed, 'Don't panic!' at him. It made Freddie feel a little better and he thought, *I will just try my best*.

Around him everyone was frantically busy, **WHIPPING** and **CREAMING**, **BEATING** and **ICING**, as things got tenser and tenser and the minutes ticked away. First Samuel dropped a bowl of icing all over the floor and then

about ten minutes later there was a
howl of frustration from Jojo.

'That's my second load of custard
to curdle!' she cried.

Freddie did his best to remain calm.
Once the new cakes were in the oven,

he got busy making the icing. He carefully added in a few drops of the pink colouring. It smelled beautifully of raspberries, and it really did give the most **LOVELY** pink colour. *Well that's one good thing*, Freddie thought, feeling his spirits lift a little.

'So young man, what are you making today?' Monsieur Brioche asked, appearing by his side.

'A cake based on the carousel in the park,' Freddie replied.

Monsieur Brioche gasped and his face lit up like a candle.

'How fantastique! But very difficult, my friend, very difficult.'

'I know,' Freddie agreed, feeling even more nervous.

'And this is the pink icing for it? It looks just the right colour. May I try it?' Monsieur Brioche asked.

'Of course,' Freddie replied.

Monsieur Brioche stuck his finger into the icing and then put it into his mouth. He pulled a face.

'Oh dear! That is **TERRIBLE**—really bad. I do not know what you have put in there, my friend, but something has gone **VERY** wrong!'

Monsieur Brioche walked off to talk to Jojo leaving Freddie in a cold sweat of panic. He tried the icing, and to his horror, he found that Monsieur Brioche was right—it was **DISGUSTING**—it tasted like soap mixed with cheese.

How on earth has that happened?! he thought frantically. In a terrible fluster he tried the icing sugar, but that tasted fine. *Perhaps one of the eggs was rotten?* he thought, dipping his finger into the bowl where he had whipped them. No, nothing wrong with them. *It couldn't be the lemon juice,* he thought but he tried it all the same, and the glycerine, which only left the pink food colouring. He put a drop on his finger and then put it in his mouth.

EUUCCHH! Freddie had to stop himself spitting it out, it tasted so revolting. But why in the world would that old man sell him something so disgusting? Was it some kind of trick?

Poor Freddie! He looked at the clock and saw that the minutes were slipping away and the cakes would barely be done in time, and even if they were, he had no icing to put on them. It was a **CATASTROPHE** and Freddie felt like giving up and going home. But then a kind voice said to him, 'Don't worry Freddie, your cakes look like they're rising beautifully.'

Mrs Mackenzie had come over as she had seen what had happened, and could also see how upset Freddie was. She gave his arm a comforting squeeze and said, 'Borrow my pink food colouring if you like. It's not raspberry-flavoured, but at least it's the right colour.' And she passed him her bottle.

Freddie felt as if he was drowning and someone had thrown him a lifejacket. Mrs Mackenzie was right, the cakes did look like they were cooking nicely and would be ready in time. And if he had some pink colouring, although his cake wouldn't taste so strongly of raspberries, it would at least be the right colour.

'Are you sure you don't mind lending it to me?' Freddie asked.

'Of course not. I know you'd do the same for me,' Mrs Mackenzie smiled kindly. 'Do you have enough icing sugar and other ingredients?'

'Yes, I do and thank you so much. You're such a good friend,' Freddie replied, giddy with relief. He looked out at the audience and Amira gave him a thumbs up and an encouraging smile.

Bernard however, wasn't happy . . .

'Excuse me! Mrs Van de Lune! Monsieur Brioche! Could you come over here, please!' Bernard called out. He was looking **VERY** cross.

The pair went over to his workstation.

'You know, I hate to do this, but I think I have to draw your attention to some cheating,' Bernard said.

'Cheating?!' Monsieur Brioche cried, looking alarmed.

'Mrs Mackenzie is lending Freddie

ingredients. And I'm sure that's not allowed under competition rules. It said on the poster that contestants must provide their own ingredients.'

Mrs Van de Lune thought for a moment.

'No, I think that's fine. We can allow that,' she said, smiling at Mrs Mackenzie and Freddie.

'But Mrs Van de Lune,' Bernard protested, 'if it said on the poster . . .'

'Mr Macaroon!' Mrs Van de Lune cut him off and looked at him fiercely. 'There is nothing in the rules, which *I* wrote by the way, saying that contestants

can't help each other. Now I suggest
you be quiet and get on with your *own*
cake.'

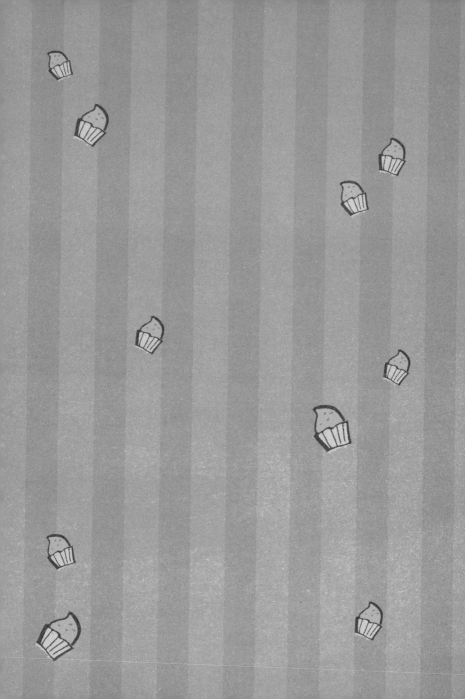

CHAPTER SEVEN

Bernard was so cross that he practically had smoke coming out of his ears, but Freddie didn't notice. He was totally focused on finishing his cake. It only felt like a couple of minutes later that Mrs Van de Lune announced,

'Twenty minutes to go bakers!'

'Oh no!' Jojo cried, nearly dropping her tart as she took it out of the oven.

Samuel's hand shook so much that his piping bag zig-zagged icing all over his cake.

Mrs Mackenzie tutted to herself while she concentrated on adding the finishing touches to her cherry blossom biscuits. And Bernard struggled to keep calm and stop his hand from shaking as he piped 'Van de Lune's Hotel' onto his cake.

Freddie took a deep breath and put his sponges into the freezer to finish cooling while he started moulding the horses.

'Ten minutes to go bakers!'

Freddie whipped the cakes out of the freezer and sandwiched them together with buttercream. *They look OK*, he thought as he started to pile the new pink icing onto the cakes as fast as he could, using the flat of a knife to smooth it down.

'Five minutes to go bakers!'

Freddie was beginning to seriously panic—he was never going to finish in time. Why on earth did he ever think he could do this! Then, as if by magic, Jojo appeared by his side.

'My apple tart is all done—is there anything I can do to help?' she asked.

'Oh, thank you so much!' Freddie said. 'Please could you finish putting the pink icing on? Then I can get on with the decorations.'

They both got busy, but too soon Mrs Van de Lune was saying,

'Three minutes to go!'

Flapjack gave a bark of encouragement as Freddie completed the roses, putting a gold ball in the middle of each.

'Two minutes to go! Just two minutes!' Mrs Van de Lune cried.

The pink icing was on, and Jojo was busy smoothing it with a knife while Freddie began to put the marzipan decorations around the top of the carousel.

'One minute!'

'Come on!' Freddie told himself as he began on the roses. He hadn't quite finished when Mrs Van de Lune said,

'Thirty seconds to go!'

They'll have to do, Freddie thought as
he and Jojo picked up the horses
on the poles and began to push
them into the cake. One, two,
three went in.

'Come on, Freddie!'
Amira called from the
audience. But Freddie
didn't hear; he was
concentrating so
intensely on the
horses.

Nearly there, he thought to himself, carefully placing the top layer onto the cake, *nearly there* . . .

'Time's up, bakers! Step away from your cakes now, please!'

Monsieur Brioche cried.

Freddie let out a long sigh of relief; he had just finished in time. Amira gave him a thumbs up.

'Well done!' said Jojo and Mrs Mackenzie.

'I couldn't have done it without your help,' he said. 'Thank you, you really are great friends.'

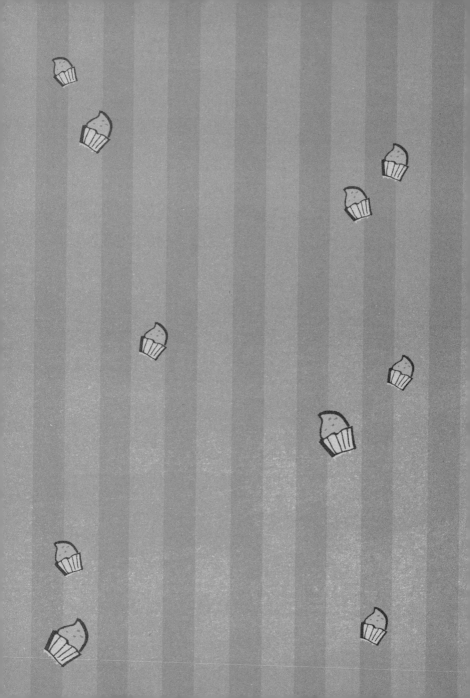

CHAPTER EIGHT

Phew! That was all pretty tense wasn't
it? And now things are about to get
EVEN MORE TENSE because it's time for
THE JUDGING!

Mrs Van de Lune and
Monsieur Brioche
began with Jojo and
her apple pie.

'Well, it looks **DELICIOUS**, and Belville *is* famous for its apple orchards,' Mrs Van de Lune said. 'The pastry is a **LOVELY** golden colour.'

'And no soggy bottom!' Monsieur Brioche announced, cutting into it, and the audience all laughed. Jojo held her breath as they tried it.

'**DELICIOUS!**' Mrs Van de Lune announced.

Monsieur Brioche slowly chewed the tart with a look of great concentration on his face. Poor Jojo thought she might faint with nerves. Will he like it? she wondered, along with the rest of the audience. After what felt like hours of chewing, Monsieur Brioche swallowed and said, '**EXQUISITE.**'

Jojo breathed and grinned with relief.

But Monsieur Brioche hadn't finished,
'I love the juicy raisins,' he said. 'And it
has just the right amount of cinnamon.
FANTASTIQUE!'

They left a beaming Jojo and moved on
to Samuel.

Samuel had made
a model of the most
famous bridge in
Belville, complete
with a canal beneath
it with boats on it.
'Isn't that
AMAZING?!'

Monsieur Brioche cried.

'Very impressive,' Mrs Van de Lune
agreed. 'It seems a shame to cut it, but
we have to try it.'

The cake was cut and they both tried a small piece. But this time there was an instant reaction, and not a good one, as poor Samuel had mixed up his salt and sugar.

'It can happen to anyone,' Mrs Van de Lune said kindly while discreetly spitting the cake into her handkerchief. Monsieur Brioche washed his down with a glass of water and a shiver.

Next they went over to Mrs
Mackenzie.

'A cherry blossom
biscuit tree, how
CHARMING!' Monsieur
Brioche exclaimed.

'Very pretty!' Mrs
Van de Lune agreed.

'Now, before I try
some could you please confirm that
you haven't mixed up the salt and
sugar?' Monsieur Brioche joked and the
audience laughed. Poor Samuel went
even redder. Mrs Mackenzie smiled and
replied that she was almost certain that
she hadn't. So Monsieur Brioche and
Mrs Van de Lune both ate a piece of the
biscuit, crunching delicately away.

'Mmm, very tasty. Well done,' Mrs Van de Lune said.

Monsieur Brioche paused again, chewing and considering.

'Delicious! Congratulations!' Monsieur Brioche cried, and Mrs Mackenzie breathed a sigh of relief.

And then they moved on to Bernard.

'You know,' Monsieur Brioche began, 'when I first came to Belville from Paris as a young chef, I fell in love with those almond biscuits that your father was so famous for.' And Monsieur Brioche smacked his lips at the memory. 'Mmm! They were just so full of flavour. I'm looking forward to tasting something from the kitchen of Macaroon Patisserie again! So now, tell me, what have you made for us today, Bernard?'

'It is a model of Van de Lune's Hotel, as that represents the very best of Belville for me,' Bernard gushed.

'Well, that's very flattering,' Mrs Van de Lune replied as she looked at the cake properly. 'And it is a perfect copy of the hotel, I can see. I love the gold lettering and, oh look! You even have the drain pipes in the right place—how amazing!'

Bernard went a little pink at the compliment and looked delighted.

'It certainly looks fantastic,' Monsieur Brioche agreed. 'Sorry to ruin your masterpiece!' he joked as he cut into the cake.

'The sponge is a perfect texture,' Monsieur Brioche said when he had cut two slices.

'I agree; it appears as light as a
feather,' Mrs Van de Lune replied,
spearing a bit of cake onto her fork and
putting it in her mouth.

Bernard waited anxiously as they
chewed, both with a slightly puzzled look
on their faces.

'What flavour is it supposed to be?'

Mrs Van de Lune asked.

Bernard swallowed, looking nervous. 'It's plum and vanilla.'

'Hmm, I'm not really getting that, I'm afraid. Maybe just a tiny bit of vanilla coming through . . .' Mrs Van de Lune said.

Bernard looked hopefully at Monsieur Brioche, willing him to say something nice . . .

'I'm sorry, my friend, I am not getting any taste at all,' Monsieur Brioche replied.

Bernard looked like he might cry, so Mrs Van de Lune said, 'but well done anyway. It certainly *looks* very impressive.'

Then they walked over to Freddie's
counter.

'Oh, it's the carousel from the
park!' Mrs Van de Lune exclaimed with
delight. 'When I was a child, my absolute
favourite treat was to go for a ride on this
carousel. And I have to say, young man,
you have made the most brilliant copy—
the detailing is exquisite.'

'It most certainly is!' Monsieur Brioche said, examining the cake carefully. 'The colour, the roses, the horses—it all looks fantastic. But let us see what it tastes like.'

The cake was cut, and both judges took a bite. Freddie had never felt so nervous in his life—he was sure that without the added raspberry flavour from the icing it would be as tasteless as Bernard's.

'**PERFECTLY SCRUMPTIOUS,**' Mrs Van de Lune pronounced. 'The sponge is light and tastes **DELICIOUSLY** of raspberries and vanilla, the buttercream is really zingy, the marzipan really almond-y. Well done!'

'Oh, thank you!' Freddie cried.

'You're very welcome,' Mrs Van de Lune replied.

But Monsieur Brioche was still munching with a faraway look in his eyes. Everyone in the hall was on the edge of their seat waiting to hear what he said. After what felt like the longest minute in history, Monsieur Brioche began to speak.

'Freddie,' he began, 'when I was a boy in Paris, my grandmother used to take me once a year to the famous Café Lore as a very special treat. There I was allowed to order any one of their exquisite cakes, but I always chose their raspberry gateau because I loved it so much. And you know what? Your cake tastes exactly the same— it is superb! **MAGNIFIQUE!** Thank you for taking me back to my childhood!'

Freddie went bright red and mumbled thank you to Monsieur Brioche. Amira

gave him a massive grin and thumbs up
from the audience.

'So Monsieur Brioche and I have tasted
all the cakes now,' Mrs Van de Lune
began. 'And I think that everyone
deserves a round of applause.' The
audience all clapped and cheered. When
they were silent, she went on. 'But there
can only be one winner, and now there
will be a short break while Monsieur
Brioche and I decide who that will be.
And to keep you entertained while we are
gone, here is the Belville school choir!'

Monsieur Brioche and Mrs Van de
Lune went off, and about ten children
took their place at the front of the

stage. They were very good at singing, but nobody could really concentrate—everyone was too desperate to know who had won the competition.

Five minutes later the judges returned. The contestants all exchanged nervous smiles, except Bernard that is. He was looking pale and sweaty and deadly serious.

'Well, I think you should all be congratulated,' Monsieur Brioche began. 'Every entry was **EXCELLENT** in its own way. But there can only be one winner. Mrs Van de Lune and I both agreed that one contestant really shone—the bake itself not only tasted delicious but looked amazing.'

It's going to be Jojo or Mrs Mackenzie,

Freddie thought.

'So now the moment you've all been waiting for,' Mrs Van de Lune said. She paused before going on. The atmosphere in the hall was so tense that it felt like a rubber band about to snap. 'The winner of the first Belville baking competition is . . .' she stopped again, and Freddie could hardly breathe.

'FREDDIE AND HIS AMAZING CAROUSEL!'

An almighty cheer went up from the audience, and Freddie thought he would faint with surprise and pleasure. He couldn't believe that after all the disasters and nearly giving up that he had won!

But uh oh, Bernard was not smiling. Not at all.

'But that's not fair! He cheated!' Bernard bellowed like a furious toddler, pointing at Freddie.

Everyone fell silent.

'How did he cheat?' Monsieur Brioche asked.

'Jojo helped him!' Bernard replied. 'He never would have finished on time otherwise.'

Monsieur Brioche exchanged glances with Mrs Van de Lune.

'That is not called cheating. That is called *helping*. There is nothing in the rules about it, Mr Macaroon,' Mrs Van de Lune said in a very strict voice. 'And before you accuse anyone else of cheating, I would think very carefully. I happened to be in the Baker's Emporium yesterday afternoon when you bought up their entire stock of pink food colouring as well as several bottles of their terrible tasting joke food flavouring. Would you like to say anything about that?'

Oh dear, Bernard did not like being

told off by Mrs Van de Lune. He went bright red with fury and shouted,

'How dare you! This is what I think of your stupid competition and your stupid hotel!' And he got his cake of Van de Lune's Hotel and threw it on the ground. Even worse, he stamped up and down all over it, until it was a horrible cake-y mess, before storming out of the hall.

Well, what a drama! As you can imagine, everyone in the audience who had been silent, mouths open in surprise, all started talking at once.

But Mrs Van de Lune held up her hand and everyone was quiet.

'Let us not give Mr Macaroon another thought,' she said, turning back to

Freddie. 'Congratulations! I'm delighted to present you with this beautiful trophy and a cheque for £500!' She handed him an envelope and a LARGE silver cup which was engraved with Winner of Belville Baking Competition.

'Thank you so much!' Freddie exclaimed, unable to take it all in. He looked at Amira who was beaming. *I can get that new oven now*, he thought. But then he looked at Flapjack and thought about all the dogs at the shelter and changed his mind. 'I would like to donate my prize money to Mrs Mackenzie for the dog shelter,' he said.

Mrs Mackenzie looked amazed.

'Are you sure, Freddie?' she asked.

'Absolutely,' Freddie replied. 'I could

never have completed my cake without you, and besides, I know the shelter needs the money more than me.'

'Well, on behalf of all the dogs, thank you very much,' she said.

'That is very generous of you,' said Mrs Van de Lune. She turned to the audience. 'I think you'll agree—he's a very kind young man. Let's give him a **BIG** round of applause.'

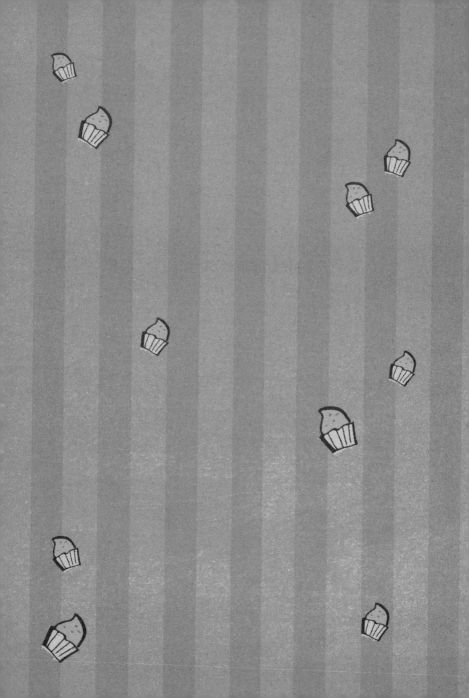

CHAPTER
NINE

Outside the hotel, everyone was
congratulating Freddie and slapping him
on the back, but he couldn't help but feel
a bit flat. He did desperately need a new
cooker.

'You did the right thing,' Amira said
kindly. 'Shall I help you carry the cake
back to the shop? You must put it in the
window—it will look **AMAZING!**'

As they turned to leave, Mrs Van de Lune appeared.

'Congratulations again, Freddie,' she said. 'Now I have a small confession to make. When I arranged the competition, I did have something else in mind too. You see Monsieur Brioche is returning to Paris, and I need to find someone else to make all the cakes and patisseries for Van de Lune's. I have met with a few people, but none of them were good enough, so in desperation I decided to organize the competition and see if I could find anyone else. And I did.' She beamed at Freddie. 'So, young man, would you be interested in becoming the patisserie chef at Van de Lune's Hotel?'

Freddie was amazed.

'That's so kind of you, Mrs Van de Lune,' Freddie said. 'But do you really think I'm good enough?'

'Absolutely,' Mrs Van de Lune replied.

Freddie thought again. To make the cakes for Van de Lune's would be such an honour. And really fun too. But there was one problem . . .

'I'm sorry, but I love my little bakery too much to ever leave it.'

Mrs Van de Lune looked disappointed, but Amira piped up, 'Would it be possible for Freddie to make the cakes at the bakery and then deliver them to the hotel?'

Mrs Van de Lune thought for a moment. 'I don't see why not. But do you have a big enough kitchen?'

'I think so, but we would need a new cooker,' Amira said.

Freddie was really worried that Mrs Van de Lune would think this was rather cheeky, but she simply replied, 'Of course, that's no problem.' She turned to Freddie, saying, 'So Freddie, what do you think?'

'That sounds PERFECT,' he said. 'Thank you.'

'We have a deal then?' Mrs Van de Lune asked.

'Yes, we most certainly do,' Freddie replied happily, and they shook hands.

The cakes Freddie made for Mrs Van
de Lune's hotel were a **GREAT** success,
and the queue outside his bakery
grew even longer, and Freddie's
baking became even more **AMAZING**.
And Bernard? Well, I would like to
be able to tell you that Bernard
changed into a really nice person,
who was kind to his staff and not
at all jealous of Freddie. However,
I would be lying if I did! But I don't
want to leave you thinking about
bad-tempered Bernard. Instead I want
you to imagine Freddie, cycling
around Belville delivering cakes with
Flapjack. And maybe, if you're lucky,
he might deliver one of his amazing
cakes to you . . .

Harriet Whitehorn grew up in London where she still lives with her family. She is the author of the Violet series (nominated for several awards including the Waterstones Children's Book Prize) and also the fantasy duo, *The Company of Eight* and *The Conspiracy of Magic*.

Alex G Griffiths is an illustrator specializing in children's picture books and character design. The majority of his work is done by hand, using a combination of pen and ink line work and brush textures in a messy way to create a natural style of illustration.

GLOSSARY

BAKE to bake food is to cook it in an oven, especially bread or cakes

BATTER a mixture of flour, eggs, and milk beaten together and used to make pancakes or to coat food before you fry it

BEAT to beat a cooking mixture is to stir it quickly so that it becomes thicker

BOIL to boil a liquid is to heat it until it starts to bubble

BRIOCHE a light sweet bread typically in the form of a small round roll

BUTTERCREAM a soft mixture of butter and icing sugar used as a filling or topping for a cake

CAKE sweet food made from a baked mixture of flour, eggs, fat, and sugar

CROISSANT a crescent-shaped roll made from rich pastry

DOUGH a thick mixture of flour and water used for making bread or pastry

ECLAIR a finger-shaped cake of pastry with a cream filling

FONDANT ICING a thick icing made from water and sugar

GATEAU a rich cream cake

GLACÉ ICING a thin icing made with icing sugar and water

MARZIPAN a soft sweet food made from almonds and sugar

MELT to melt something solid is to make it liquid by heating it

MERINGUE a crisp cake made from the whites of eggs mixed with sugar and baked

MIX to mix different things is to stir or shake them together to make one thing

MIXTURE something made of different things mixed together

MOULD to mould something is to make it have a particular shape

PASTRY a dough made from flour, fat, and water rolled flat and baked

PROFITEROLE a small ball of soft, sweet pastry filled with cream and covered with chocolate sauce

ROYAL ICING hard white icing made from icing sugar and egg whites, typically used to decorate fruit cakes

SPONGE a soft lightweight cake or pudding

STIR to stir something liquid or soft is to move it round and round, especially with a spoon

TART a tart is a pie containing fruit, jam, custard, or treacle

WHISK to whisk eggs or cream is to beat them until they are thick or frothy

FREDDIE'S
RASPBERRY CUPCAKES

YOU WILL NEED AN ASSISTANT. SO MAKE SURE THAT AN ADULT HELPS YOU!

There's no need to use food colouring for these tasty raspberry-pink treats!

INGREDIENTS

FOR THE CAKES
150g unsalted butter

150g golden caster sugar

3 large eggs

150g self-raising flour

100g frozen raspberries

FOR THE TOPPING
25g unsalted butter

75g cream cheese

1 tbsp raspberry jam

400g icing sugar

12 frozen raspberries for decoration

METHOD

1 Pre-heat the oven to 180°c (fan 160°c, gas mark 4). Line a 12-hole cupcake pan with paper cases.

2 Mix together the BUTTER and GOLDEN CASTER SUGAR until light and fluffy.

3 Add the eggs into the mixture one by one, along with a spoonful of flour.

4 Add the rest of the flour to the bowl and mix everything together.

5 Now it's time to add your raspberries, then give your mixture another good stir.

6 Fill each paper case with cupcake mixture so that they're 2/3rds full.

7 Bake in the oven for 20-25 minutes until well- risen and golden. Transfer to a wire rack and leave to cool.

8 To prepare the buttercream topping, mix the butter with the cream cheese and then add the jam.

9 Sift in the icing sugar and give your buttercream topping another stir.

10 Add a nice big splodge of buttercream topping to each cupcake and then pop a raspberry on top.

VOILA!

Here are some other great stories we think you'll love!

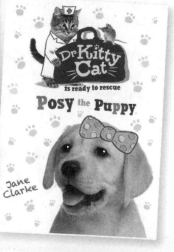